BATMAN

Hot and Cold

By Devan Aptekar

Based on the teleplays
"The Big Heat" by Christopher Yost and J. D. Murray
and "The Big Chill" by Greg Weisman

BATMAN created by Bob Kane

SCHOLASTIC INC.

New York Toronto London Auckland Sydney
Mexico City New Delhi Hong Kong Buenos Aires

This book belongs to
Mrs. Laurie Elliott
Park Avenue Elementary
Auburn, ME

ISBN 0-439-72781-2

Published by Scholastic Inc. SCHOLASTIC and associated logos are trademarks and/or
registered trademarks of Scholastic Inc.

12 11 10 9 8 7 6 5 4 3 2 1   5 6 7 8 9 10/0

Printed in the U.S.A.
First printing, September 2005

Before there was a Boy Wonder, or even a Commissioner Gordon, there was Batman.

Batman will stop at nothing to protect Gotham City from danger. His secret identity: young billionaire Bruce Wayne, the honorary head of Wayne Enterprises. Hunted by the police as well as bizarre villains bent on his destruction, Batman wages his war on crime, helped only by his longtime butler, Alfred.

The nights in Gotham City are long. And deadly. But criminals beware — Batman stalks the night in Gotham now, and he's here to stay.

PART ONE

THE BIG HEAT

Gotham's skies get dark so quickly once the sun goes down. It's as if night can barely wait to rush in and fill the city.

On this evening, a breeze blew gently through a large circular hole in the side of a tall skyscraper. The skyscraper was the Wagner Tech Building. The hole was unexpected.

A black cape fluttered near the hole as a figure slowly lowered itself from above, hanging from the side of the building by a thin metal strand. He swayed in the breeze.

A faint *beep* broke the silence. Inside an earpiece embedded in the figure's cowl, a Bat-wave transmission began.

"Master Bruce," crackled Alfred's voice. "Haven't we discussed not staying out late on school nights?"

Still hanging on to his Bat-grapnel with one hand, Batman ran a scanner over the smooth edges of the hole. "What's the problem, Alfred?"

"I thought it fit to remind you of your meeting with the mayor tomorrow morning. . . ." Alfred's voice trailed off for a moment. "Actually, that would be *this* morning."

Batman stared at the scanner, not really listening to his loyal friend and butler. The temperature reading had skyrocketed up to 500 degrees Fahrenheit.

"The glass has been seared," murmured Batman. "And it's still smoldering — just like at the research lab, two nights ago."

"Ah, yes," Alfred sighed. "Off you go, then."

Before Alfred could even finish his sentence, Batman ended the transmission and leaped through the hole.

Batman cast a shadow in the circle of moonlight streaming into the room. Around the circle, however, all was dark. He could barely make out the tall banks of computer servers lining the far walls.

He pressed a button on his Utility Belt and two infrared lenses clicked into place from inside his mask, covering the eyeholes. The room suddenly sharpened into focus. Heat lines scrawled through the computers, forming jagged patterns that rose toward the ceiling. The machines were scorched, smoking, burned out.

Batman wasn't surprised. There had also been equipment burned beyond repair at the research lab break-in. He walked silently forward, hoping to catch someone in the act.

He was in luck.

At the farthest edge of the huge room, his infrared lenses picked up the thermal image of a helmeted figure bending over a computer terminal. He was turned away from Batman, and a pack strapped to his back glowed white-hot in the infrared view. Whatever that pack was, it was loaded with energy.

Thunk! Thunk! Thunk! Batman sank three mini Batarangs into the wall beside the stranger's head. Startled, the man spun around to face him.

"Working late?" asked Batman. He could see the computer behind the stranger now — burned to a crisp like the others.

"The night shift. Like you, 'Batman.'" With those words, the stranger's costume powered up. Energized light wings seemed to spread out from the glowing pack, and in Batman's infrared view, the stranger's whole body became painfully bright. He blazed brighter and brighter until Batman couldn't see anything at all.

Batman staggered back and quickly switched off the infrared lenses. Any longer and he might have been blinded. When his vision cleared, he saw the man raising his arm to point a high-tech wrist laser right at him. The stranger's costume was yellow and black, his helmet was round and fitted closely to his head, and the energy from his glowing yellow pack still crackled in the air.

"I can bring the heat," bragged the stranger as his wrist laser pulsed bright yellow. Laser beams shot toward Batman. He dove to the side to avoid them. The lasers shot out through the side of the skyscraper and into the open air.

Batman grabbed on to the man, binding the laser-bearing arm against the stranger's body in a strong hold. With a shock, he felt the stranger pushing backward against him, toppling them both out through the circular hole and into the night sky.

Batman shot his Bat-grapnel at a nearby building and swung himself onto a rooftop. He watched the costumed stranger soar casually in circles around him, with his jet-pack flaring.

"You're full of surprises," said Batman.

The stranger slowed his circles, coming to a hovering standstill in the air above Batman. "I'm Firefly — get it? 'Fire' and 'fly.'" He chuckled. "Here's some more fire."

Firefly raised his arm and his laser began glowing yellow once more.

Batman immediately hurled two Batarangs at the man. The laser melted the first one in midflight, but the other one slammed into it. A massive burst of laser light blasted the entire rooftop and then faded away. Silver fuel spilled from the broken laser.

Firefly's suit flickered, its glow dimming fast. "You're gonna pay for that," he snarled. He lifted his other arm, a second laser opening out of his suit.

Beep! A display on Firefly's suit began flashing LOW FUEL. "Next time," Firefly amended.

He sped off into the night sky and was gone, leaving behind only a trail of yellow light.

Batman rose up from the scorched roof. Small flames flickered around him from the laser burst as he kneeled beside a silvery puddle of fuel.

He tapped his Utility Belt to activate the radio transmission.

"Alfred," he said. "I've met our arsonist. He targets computers. I'm not sure why."

Batman ran a gloved finger through the fuel. The silvery substance felt slick and almost elastic. It shone in the moonlight.

"Plus he has a jet-pack and laser technology like nothing I've ever . . . " Batman paused. "Alfred?"

There was no response.

Batman wiped his glove clean and raised his hand to his head. Part of his cowl had been burned off in the laser blast, exposing the sizzling wires of the two-way radio antenna.

"'Firefly,' huh?" he said to the seared rooftop.

"Don't let that photograph fool you, Bruce," said Mayor Grange, walking into the room. "I may be holding that fish, but your father's the one who caught it."

Bruce turned away from the framed photo and smiled at Mayor Grange. The two men shook hands.

"Well, Dad always did believe in charity, Mayor Grange," Bruce quipped.

Gotham's mayor laughed aloud. "Bruce, it's been too long." Grange's smile was genuine and wistful, but it faded quickly. "Come on into my office."

Bruce gave one last look at the photo of his dad and the not-yet-mayor. They seemed to be in their late twenties — Bruce's own age! — and looked happy, dressed in their fishing gear and huge galoshes. With an effort, he left the picture behind and followed after Mayor Grange.

"Unfortunately, I didn't call you here for a social visit," said the mayor gravely, moving behind his massive desk. He gestured for Bruce to sit opposite him.

"Wayne Foundation business?" asked Bruce.

"Bruce . . . there's no easy way to say this. As you know, the city is about to award the contract to rebuild and expand the children's hospital."

"Right," agreed Bruce, a little confused. "To the Wayne Foundation."

Grange took a deep breath. "The city council is leaning toward GothCorp."

"What?" Bruce was shocked.

"Bruce—" began Mayor Grange.

"Wayne Industries and the Foundation have supported the children's hospital from the beginning," interrupted Bruce. "Since my father *founded* it."

"Bruce—" the mayor tried again.

"GothCorp isn't known for its acts of public service. They're known for allegations, investigations, resignations — too many 'ations for my taste."

"Bruce, the council isn't concerned with GothCorp's reputation. They're leery of *yours*."

"Mine?" murmured Bruce, taken aback.

Mayor Grange shifted uncomfortably in his

chair. "Your public image . . . well, let's just say it doesn't inspire much confidence."

Bruce nodded heavily. The mayor got up and walked around the desk to Bruce's side.

"Look," Grange said. "Your father was one of my closest friends: I *see* him in you. But the council, they see you as, well . . . "

"A party boy?" Bruce asked.

Grange turned his head away, but Bruce stood to face him. "Mayor Grange, let *me* make the case for the Wayne Foundation. Give me the chance to convince them."

The mayor stared into Bruce's eyes.

"*Please*," said Bruce. His voice was soft but rock solid.

Mayor Grange sighed. "The council is voting on the contract tomorrow at eight A.M. sharp."

"I'll be there," said Bruce with conviction. "At the top of my game."

"And wear a tie," added the mayor.

"Eight A.M. is bright and early for you, Master Bruce," Alfred noted. The stone walls of the Batcave glowed green from the light of many computer screens. On the huge main screen, Bruce had just brought up the GothCorp Web site.

Alfred watched intently for a minute but then glanced back at Bruce. "Perhaps you should think about getting some rest."

Bruce gave a slight jerk of his head. "Not until I've gathered enough ammo regarding GothCorp's questionable business practices."

As Bruce typed, the many smaller side monitors flickered with activity. Newspaper articles, press releases, and investigative reports all flowed past. "The children's hospital was my father's personal cause, Alfred: I need to be certain I can sway the council's vote."

BEEP! BEEP! The main monitor was ablaze with a flashing Batwave signal. Information began to scroll across the screen.

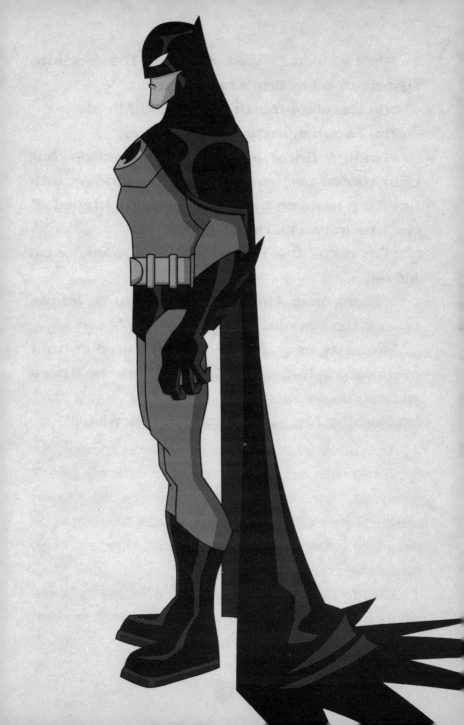

"Police alert," said Bruce. "The security system of a law firm's been tripped."

"On the sixty-fourth floor," said Alfred.

The two men exchanged a glance.

"Firefly." Bruce immediately leaped up, but then turned back to stare at the screens with GothCorp news on them. His mouth tightened. "I can't be in two places at once."

"I'm quite the researcher, you know," said Alfred.

"Thank you, Alfred," Bruce called as he ran toward the Batsuit. "I won't be long."

Moments later, he stood fully suited in front of the Whirly Bat, a modified helicopter he'd been working on for months.

"Tonight," he said, "I clip Firefly's wings."

The Whirly Bat cut silently across the Gotham sky. After smoothly maneuvering the copter around several skyscrapers, Batman pulled up next to a window on the sixty-fourth floor.

Smoke was pouring out of a perfectly circular hole in the glass.

Firefly's work, all right, thought Batman. *But a law firm doesn't fit the profile.*

Batman hit a couple of buttons on the complicated Whirly Bat dashboard. In the center of the windshield, a computerized infrared display appeared. According to the readout, there was no one inside — just a lot of smoldering cabinets and computers.

Batman punched a button to clear the infrared display and turned the Whirly Bat to face the opposite direction. He was almost startled — *almost* — to find Firefly hovering before him.

He clicked on an audio channel so he could hear if Firefly said anything incriminating. The arsonist had already shown he was a talker who liked to taunt people. Maybe he would go too far this time.

"Well, well," said Firefly, right on cue. "So the bat flies after all." His jet-pack began to glow white-hot as he zoomed forward straight at the Whirly Bat.

Batman whipped the controls hard and the copter veered to the right, narrowly avoiding Firefly as he streaked past. Firefly's light wings were almost a blur and the bright yellow of his wrist lasers was growing in intensity.

The Whirly Bat turned to face Firefly again. Firefly chuckled. "You don't really think you're going to catch me in that thing, do — "

Batman launched two arrays of stun-missiles before Firefly could complete his question.

The villain deftly avoided the attack, lasering several missiles as he danced through the air. "You," Firefly finished. He spun around and lasered the last missile grandly, only to sputter in surprise as it exploded in a cloud of tear gas, blowing him backward.

He coughed and spat, ducking under the quickly dissipating cloud. "Tear gas? I'll give you something to cry about," he growled.

The night sky was illuminated like a deadly disco, with strobe-light explosions of color. Firefly hovered in front of the Whirly Bat, shooting brilliantly sizzing laser beams all around, but not at the copter itself.

He's playing with me, thought Batman.

Firefly turned and streaked away, the Whirly Bat only seconds behind him. They zoomed through the labyrinth of skyscrapers and emerged near the docks.

Batman increased his speed, trying to catch up.

Just as Batman was nearing Firefly, the mysterious criminal stopped dead in the air for a second. Batman grabbed his controls to avoid slamming into him.

With his attention diverted for that split second, Batman was unable to react as Firefly darted upward and flicked a laser beam at the back end of the copter.

"Who's the hotshot now?" bragged Firefly.

The entire tail of the Whirly Bat fell into the river while the rest of the copter spun out of control. Batman struggled as his vehicle twisted through the air, sinking fast.

It slammed into the roof of an abandoned warehouse with a spectacular crash. On impact, dust and shards flew everywhere. In the cockpit, everything went black.

6

". . . Master Bruce? Master Bruce! Are you there? Please answer. . . ." Alfred's voice crackled over the radio transmission.

With a groan, Batman squeezed an eye half open. Where was he? His head throbbed. It felt so heavy. His shoulders were pressed uncomfortably into his cross-body seat restraints. When his blurry vision came into focus, he felt his whole world flip.

He was hanging upside down in the cockpit of the destroyed Whirly Bat. The wreckage was caught tightly in the iron girders of the warehouse roof it had crashed through.

Batman strained to free himself, but the clasps seemed to have fused somehow. "Alfred," he said groggily. His head kept throbbing.

He looked toward the ground to estimate the fall: around ten feet. Still shaky, he concentrated on getting one arm free.

"I've been trying to reach you for hours," Alfred said. "The communicator wasn't— "

"Hours?" Batman snapped to attention. He brought his head to his chest and looked past his feet. Light poured through the hole he had made in the roof. The sky was blue. Daylight blue.

"Alfred, what time is it?"

"Five minutes to *eight*, sir."

Batman took a deep breath and managed to free one arm. He quickly flipped open a Batarang and began to slice through the rest of the restraints. "Do you have the research?" Batman asked.

"In your vehicle already," crackled Alfred's voice. "Right beside a fresh change of clothes and your electric razor."

Batman dropped down from the wreckage with a flip, landing on his feet. "Don't forget the tie," he said.

Five to eight?

He pressed a button on his Utility Belt to signal his location to the Batmobile. Miles away in the Batcave, the vehicle hummed to life. Alfred was hurrying toward it, a necktie fluttering in his hand. "Wait! Wait, you blasted machine!"

With no driver, the Batmobile took off, leaving Alfred in its dust.

7

With a running start, Batman leaped off the roof of the warehouse. He had checked the Batmobile's progress and timed it perfectly. He sank into the shock-absorbing seat of the Batmobile and the hatch closed above him.

The vehicle had barely even slowed down. Now, it was speeding from alley to alley, working its way back toward the city center. Batman began pulling off his costume. He grabbed the clothes neatly folded on the seat beside him.

"Great," he grumbled. "No tie."

The Batmobile sped toward a dead end — a brick wall at the end of a deserted alleyway. It swerved to the right, under a Dumpster that rose hydraulically into the air. A secret underground passageway gaped beneath. The Batmobile shot into the darkness as the Dumpster lowered smoothly, sealing the entrance.

Seconds later, at the other end of the alley, the ground opened and a black Porsche barreled out onto the street. The concrete slab of the

sidewalk slid back into place.

Inside the Porsche, Bruce pressed hard on the accelerator, his suit roughly on, his shirt half-buttoned. He took the last few turns and pulled up in front of City Hall.

Grabbing the stack of papers and folders that Alfred had collected for him, Bruce sprinted up the stairs. High above him, the giant clock tower read 8:13. He didn't stop to see.

Bruce's footsteps echoed through the marbled lobby. He managed a half-wave to the bemused desk guards and took the final flight of stairs three at a time.

He paused for one quick breath and then opened the double doors of the city council meeting room. Bruce stepped into the room.

The council members stared at him and the room went silent. He was disheveled and still breathing heavily. They were mostly old men in black suits and many of them were getting up from their chairs at the long mahogany table.

Bruce hesitantly stepped forward and placed his pile of scattered documents on the table. He self-consciously tried to pat down his wild hair as he cleared his throat.

"Ahem. Forgive me for running late, gentlemen and lady. I, uh — had a fender-bender on the way, but I'm here now and . . . "

The council members were staring back at him, blank-faced. A few began whispering to one another. Bruce felt a hand on his shoulder.

He turned to see Mayor Grange beside him. "I'm sorry, Bruce," the mayor said. "You weren't here. The vote has already been cast."

Bruce felt his heart drop. "I see," he said quietly. He picked up his crumpled papers and let Mayor Grange lead him away from the council.

The members' voices grew spitefully louder as they crossed the room. Bruce couldn't help but make out some of the words and phrases.

"Disgrace . . . "

"Spoiled child . . . "

"Clearly out gallivanting all night . . . "

"He's no Thomas Wayne!"

At the last remark, Bruce reeled. They couldn't have said anything more painful.

8

Bruce stared glumly at the Batsuit hanging in its chamber. "I've failed twice today, Alfred."

The empty eyes of the cowl seemed to stare back at him. Bruce felt exhausted and demoralized. "As Batman *and* as Bruce Wayne."

He turned his attention to the photo he clutched in his hand — a photo of his father at the opening of the Gotham Children's Hospital. "I tried to do everything," Bruce continued, "and failed to accomplish *anything*."

Alfred moved closer, resting a hand on the Batsuit chamber. "You are, after all, only one man, Master Bruce."

Bruce frowned. "Then maybe it's time to turn Wayne Industries over to someone capable of running it. Maybe it's time to be a full-time Batman."

Alfred cocked an eyebrow. "Or a full-time Bruce Wayne," he replied, turning and walking away toward the elevator.

Bruce stood in brooding thought, looking

at the Batsuit. After a while, he reached over and clicked on some music, dark and mournful. He switched on a few TV screens as well and began pacing in front of them, waiting for news reports.

He kicked a trash can, sending it rolling across the floor. He pulled out one Batarang after another, throwing them to let off more steam. They arced around the Batcave, one piercing the can and pinning it to the floor, the rest sailing into the trash.

He noticed something and turned up the volume on one of the screens. A reporter was standing on the sidewalks of downtown Gotham.

"The latest victim in this plague of arson," she was saying, "is a law firm representing many of Gotham's industrial clients."

Bruce froze and dropped the Batarang he'd been about to throw. He quickly clicked off the music.

"The influential firm of Schnapp, Velez, and Rudikoff handled the bankruptcy cases of Gotham Telecommunications, Starr Chemical — "

Bruce paused the television and stood in silence, thinking aloud. "All those companies they represented were arson victims, too," he said. "And they all went under. And now even their law firm's been put out of business."

He sat down at the computer console and began typing. Headlines came up on the main screen: GOTHAM TELECOM DECLARES BANKRUPTCY AFTER ARSON. STARR CHEMICAL DROPS OUT AFTER ARSON.

Bruce shook his head. "But who'd profit from these companies being out of business?" He kept typing. An idea was beginning to form in his head.

The monitor went blank and then a new headline popped up beside a GothCorp logo: CITY AWARDS STARR CHEMICAL CONTRACT TO

GOTHCORP.

"GothCorp, that's who," Bruce said, smiling grimly as the realization hit him. "It was staring me in the face the whole time."

Behind him, Alfred entered the Batcave with a dinner tray in his hand. Bruce sensed his movement and turned to face him.

"Firefly doesn't commit arson, Alfred," Bruce said. "He commits corporate sabotage . . . and he's working for GothCorp!"

Alfred snorted, placing the dinner tray down before Bruce. "It's no wonder that GothCorp is so interested in funding the children's hospital."

Bruce nodded. "Nothing like good PR to distract the public from dirty business. Plus, they can launder some of their dirty money through the hospital."

"You know," said Alfred thoughtfully, "perhaps Batman and Bruce Wayne can work together to stop Firefly *and* GothCorp?"

Bruce stood up, a sly smile forming on his face. "Batman will fight fire with fire, but first—" he glanced at the freeze-frame of the smoking law-firm building — "Bruce Wayne needs to lead a certain moth to a flame."

9

"And in business news, local billionaire Bruce Wayne stepped into the spotlight again, this time with breaking news at Wayne Industries."

The apartment was dark. The only light came from the one television in the corner. A shadowy figure watched from the couch.

The news report cut to footage from earlier that day, outside the Wayne Industries building. Bruce Wayne stood behind a podium.

"I can't reveal any details yet," Bruce was saying, "but in the next few days, Wayne Industries will unveil a prototype that will make us the premier technology company in Gotham. In fact, it'll set the whole tech world on fire."

The reporter spoke up. "Aren't you concerned about competition from GothCorp?"

Bruce smiled and looked straight into the camera. "Let's just say I wouldn't want to be GothCorp right now."

Inside the apartment, the phone rang. The man reached out to grab it.

"Yeah," said the man. "I'm watching it." He glanced at the yellow-and-black helmet that sat on top of the television set and he smirked, listening to the frantic voice on the other end of the line.

"No problem," he interrupted. "Yeah, my usual rate. . . . I understand, just like the others." He grinned cruelly. "Wayne Industries is gonna go down in flames."

The laser beam traced a perfect circle in the window. Sparks of molten glass sprayed out from the edges. The wide disc of tinted shatterproof glass fell forward into the room, revealing Firefly floating outside in the night sky.

He stepped inside into the darkness. His jet-pack lit up the air around him. Suddenly, he spun around, sensing movement. Nothing was there.

He turned back to find himself facing a tall dark shadow. "Firefly," said the shadow.

Firefly was startled but assumed his usual cocky swagger. "Well, Batman," he sneered. "I see you survived your copter crack-up."

"I know about GothCorp," said Batman impassively.

Firefly cocked his head. "What's that, a rock band or something?"

"For someone who gets his kicks scorching tech companies, I find it hard to believe you've never heard of them."

In response, Firefly powered up his wrist laser,

turning the room yellow with its glow. Batman hurled a Batarang and knocked Firefly's arm off course. A beam sliced through the ceiling.

Batman leaned in. "You're finished, Firefly," he said. "Cooked."

"Says who?" responded Firefly with an arrogant chuckle. He turned and dove for the window. His jet-pack ignited as he sailed through the circular hole.

Firefly twisted in midair to face the building. Batman stood just inside the large hole. "No one touches me in the sky," bellowed Firefly.

Batman swept off his cape, letting it fall smoothly to the floor. Strapped to his back was a bat-styled jet-pack to rival Firefly's own. Firefly gasped involuntarily. "Whoa," he muttered.

"This time, *I* brought the heat," said Batman. His Batpack ignited with a small roar and Batman flew cleanly through the hole. He slammed into Firefly's chest. Firefly went spinning toward a building but righted himself at the last minute. Batman streaked toward him.

Firefly opened fire with his lasers, but Batman avoided them with ease. Firefly grinned, clearly enjoying the challenge. "Handles nice," he said.

"But does it have horsepower?"

He sped off, a streak of yellow light in the gloomy Gotham night. Batman raced after him.

Now two streaks of light cut across the sky, one yellow and one blue. They swerved up and down, weaving between buildings and around them. Batman inched close to try and grab Firefly's jet-pack but had to pull away as Firefly turned and fired laser beams at him.

With a smirk back at Batman, Firefly went into a nosedive. He shot down toward the street. Batman rocketed after him. A cabbie yelped to see the two figures zooming toward his car. He ducked instinctively against his seat. They finally pulled up, narrowly avoiding the taxicab.

The cabbie pulled over to the side. "Yikes," he said to his passenger. "And I thought Metropolis was bad."

Meanwhile, Firefly was weaving through traffic with Batman in hot pursuit. He turned and fired back at Batman. Batman dodged the laser but saw it tear through the trailer of a truck behind him.

This is too dangerous, thought Batman. *I've got to stop him before someone gets hurt.*

Batman thought fast as he soared through the air after him. He reached down and pulled out his Bat-grapnel and fired it forward, catching Firefly's leg. Firefly spun around, firing his lasers wildly.

One of the beams severed the grapnel line, freeing Firefly. Still speeding forward, Firefly looked up in time to see that they were about to slam into the top of a tunnel entrance.

Batman ducked into the tunnel, slowing down to check that no cars had been hit by lasers. Satisfied, he sped up to try and catch Firefly once more. But as he concentrated on staying above the cars and below the roof of the tunnel, Batman didn't notice Firefly waiting for him outside, both lasers raised and aimed.

11

The laser beams shot at Batman just as he emerged from the tunnel. He spun in the air, avoiding the first beam.

Zap! The second beam tagged his Bat-pack. With a jerk, Batman felt himself being pulled off course. He made a last effort and lurched forward, slamming hard into Firefly.

The two of them grappled as they flew higher and higher, with smoke rising from the side of the Bat-pack. Batman delivered a punch. With his other hand, he ripped the fuel cables out of Firefly's jet-pack.

They fell hard onto a rooftop. Batman rolled with the fall and came up on his feet, flicking open a Batarang.

"Last chance, Firefly," he said.

Firefly scrambled to his feet, raising a wrist laser to point at Batman. His suit was smeared with silver fuel leaking from the cables. Before he could fire, the glow in his suit flickered and went dull. No juice.

"You're empty," said Batman, with the barest hint of a smile. He unstrapped his Bat-pack and let it fall to the graveled rooftop. He dropped the Batarang beside it. It hit the ground with a clank. "Just you and me," he said.

Firefly rushed at Batman, finally losing his cocky cool. Batman deftly stepped to the side, grabbing Firefly's arm and slamming him to the roof with his own momentum.

Firefly swept Batman's legs out from under him and quickly got to his feet as Batman handspringed backwards. "No one . . . touches me . . . " said Firefly through gritted teeth.

" ' . . . In the sky?'" finished Batman, quoting Firefly from outside Wayne Industries. He gestured down at the rooftop surface on which they now stood.

Firefly charged at Batman again, unleashing a series of punches and kicks, all of which Batman dodged and deflected with ease, barely moving.

With great effort and a loud scream, Firefly sent a huge roundhouse kick toward Batman's head.

Batman caught his foot and spun it, sending Firefly slamming back into the gravel.

This last impact shattered Firefly's mask, and a chunk of black glass fell out onto the rooftop. An eye blinked heavily behind the mask. Firefly was breathing very hard.

"Face facts," said Batman as he approached. "You've been burned."

12

A newspaper slammed down on the long mahogany table. The front-page photo showed Firefly tied up in front of the GothCorp Building, his shattered helmet beside him. A sign strapped to his chest read GOTHCORP EMPLOYEE OF THE MONTH.

The headline above the photo was: GOTHCORP IMPLICATED IN FIREFLY ARSONS.

Mayor Grange and the city council members stood around the paper, staring quietly. The usually stern, disapproving council members now looked uncomfortable and embarrassed.

The mayor of Gotham cleared his throat. "Well, based on recent, er . . . facts that have come to light . . . " He glanced at Bruce Wayne, refreshed and very well put together at his side. This time, Bruce even wore a necktie.

"I suggest," Mayor Grange continued, "that the council recast their vote on the matter of the children's hospital, as well as on *all* contracts currently held by GothCorp."

The council members grunted and mumbled their agreement, exchanging embarrassed looks.

Mayor Grange turned to Bruce and spoke in a low voice so that no one else would hear. "Bruce, your father would be proud of you if he were here today."

Bruce smiled sadly, moved by the compliment.

But he tried to make a joke out of it instead, to distract himself from the emotion that welled up inside. "Mayor," he said, "I like to think there's more to me than a good-looking tie."

PART TWO

THE BIG CHILL

13

The Gotham night was hot. Too hot. Summers in Gotham got so sweltering and thick, residents felt like they could barely breathe.

Out on Gotham Bay, a luxury yacht motored quietly through the sticky darkness. A fancy party was going on inside, but three silhouettes could be seen on the deck.

"I imagined that jetting out on the bay would be certain escape from this grueling heat wave," complained the middle-aged man in an expensive tuxedo.

His diamond-draped wife nodded absently, eyeing the young movie star beside her.

"I'm afraid if the mercury rises any higher," continued the man, "my only option will be to take *this* little angel for a dance." He draped his arm around a large dripping ice sculpture of a cherub.

"Now, darling," responded his wife. "You don't want me getting jealous."

"It's only fair, love. I had to watch you dance

with that Wayne chap at the charity ball."

The movie star spun around excitedly. "Bruce Wayne?" she asked. "Is he here?"

"No," scoffed the man. "Mr. Wayne only does charity functions."

"He's too tragically hip for the likes of us," added his wife, twirling a strand of diamonds. The three of them huddled together, forgetting the heat for a moment as they gossiped about Bruce Wayne.

Inside, the young first mate held the wheel tightly and stared nervously ahead of him. "Uh, Skipper," he said to the captain. "What's our procedure in case of an . . . iceberg?"

The captain was holding a plate of hors d'oeuvres he had snuck from the party below. He turned to the mate with his mouth still full. "An *iceberg*? In Gotham Bay? In this heat? My boy, I guarantee we don't . . . ."

His voice trailed off into a moment of wide-eyed silence. The captain finally lurched for the wheel and spun it desperately, trying to turn the ship. "Mayday!" he shouted. "Mayday!"

It was too late. The iceberg had seemingly bloomed out of nowhere and the yacht had too much momentum to react in time. The yacht slammed into the iceberg and stuck fast.

The movie star and the couple lay sprawled on the deck as the captain and the mate rushed from the bridge. While the captain helped them back to their feet, the mate ran to calm the passengers in the cabin below.

A strange sound distracted them. It was a soft whooshing, low and rhythmic. The captain looked up and gasped. Someone, some*thing*, was coming toward them, stepping off the iceberg and onto the yacht.

"Weather's a bit . . . muggy," the cold, gravelly voice intoned.

The creepy figure was tall and wore a full bodysuit from shoulder to boots. His head was encased in a jagged glassy helmet, his face obscured in a haze within. Red eyes glowed through.

The stranger walked across the deck. Thin patches of ice formed under his feet as he moved.

The man in the tuxedo stepped toward him, outraged. "You are not welcome here, Mister . . . uh, Mister . . . ?"

"Freeze will do," intoned the stranger, raising one arm.

"Well, Mr. Freeze," snarled the millionaire, "you do not have permission to come aboard – "

A blast of icy mist and snow burst out from the palm of Mr. Freeze's gloved hand,

completely encasing the sputtering man in a massive block of ice.

The movie star screamed in horror. "What do you want?"

Mr. Freeze walked closer. "Ice," he said simply. When no one responded, he shrugged and pulled out a small silver ice pick.

"I-I don't understand," the wife stammered. She looked frantically around from Freeze to the movie star to the captain, clutching her diamond necklaces to her chest.

Mr. Freeze pressed a small button on the handle of the ice pick and its tip began to emit a high-pitched sonic pulse. "Think about it," he said. "Think fast."

He turned away from the frozen millionaire and instead jabbed the tip of his ice pick into the cherub ice sculpture on the table. It shattered explosively, spraying ice chunks across the deck.

Mr. Freeze now unzipped a small satchel and held it open. "The ice," he demanded.

The two women looked at each other and then began throwing their diamond jewelry into the bag. Mr. Freeze nodded and stomped forward into the cabin full of wealthy partygoers below.

Several minutes later, he emerged. His satchel was almost overflowing with diamonds. He zipped it closed and slung it over his back.

"Have an ice evening," Mr. Freeze intoned.

He walked past the man still encased in ice and hopped nimbly over the yacht railing, freezing a path across the water for himself as he strode toward Gotham City.

15

"All crime fighting and no play," said Alfred, "makes Master Bruce an extremely dull boy."

Bruce was tinkering with the still-destroyed frame of the Whirly Bat, pulling singed wires out and replacing them with new ones. He didn't respond.

Alfred pressed his point. "Even Batman deserves to go on holiday once in a while, wouldn't you say?"

"Alfred," said Bruce. "You know how stir-crazy I'd be, lying on some beach."

Alfred smiled. "Which is why I've arranged for an *athletic* retreat — a way to hone Batman's body and reflexes." He lifted up a highly polished pair of skis. "Not to mention escaping this heat wave."

Bruce looked back from the skis to Alfred and sighed. "You've booked reservations, haven't you?"

Alfred shrugged ever so slightly.

"Well, I'll think about it," said Bruce. "But

if I go, it's only to make you happy."

Suddenly, the Bat-wave alert came buzzing up on the main monitor. Bruce leaped toward the console to see what was going on. An image came up on the screen: a news reporter on the docks of Gotham Harbor. Bruce switched on the sound.

" . . . The mind-boggling jewelry theft here at Gotham Harbor has left one man *frozen solid* – not to mention an actual iceberg floating in Gotham Bay! At present, little is known of the bizarre perpetrator calling himself Mr. Freeze."

"There, you see: It's a sign," said Alfred dryly. "A winter retreat is in your future."

Bruce smiled. He dropped the wiring tools and sprinted off to grab his Batsuit, leaving Alfred behind to put away the skis.

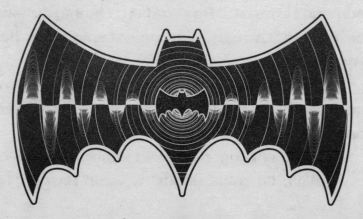

16

Police cars were stationed all around the dock, their red lights giving the night a cherry tint. The block of ice containing the frozen millionaire had been towed to shore by the paramedics. They had mostly thawed him out, surrounding him with massive space heaters. Now they draped layers of blankets over his upper body and turned their attention to freeing his legs.

Detective Ethan Bennett walked up to the chief paramedic. "Is he going to be all right?"

"He's hypothermic, but he'll pull through."

"No th-thanks to that maniac," interjected the millionaire through chattering teeth.

"So how'd he do it?" asked Bennett.

The paramedic turned up his hands. "I'm really not sure. But the victim appears to have been, uhhh, flash-frozen."

Bennett shook his head in disbelief and joined his partner, Detective Ellen Yin. She was questioning the captain.

"He walked on *water*?" she repeated.

"Well, he froze it first," said the captain.

"Made a path of solid ice, straight to the shore."

Yin glanced at Bennett. "No sign of that now," she said.

"Trail's gone cold," said Bennett. Yin glared at him. "Er, so to speak," he amended, kicking gently at the worn wood of the dock.

In the darkness below the dock, Batman clung to a wooden pylon, half-submerged in water. He was holding a mini-radar-microphone.

"Trail wasn't quite cold *enough*," said Yin. "Not in this weather."

Batman flicked his wrist to collapse the listening device and slid it into a slot on his Utility Belt. *Not cold enough for the naked eye,* he thought.

He climbed along beneath the dock until he reached the crumbling, abandoned edge. Infrared lenses swiveled down inside his cowl to cover his eyes. He poked his head up, protected by shadows.

The ice-blue footsteps leading away from the dock were clear as crystal.

17

From a distance, everything seemed quiet at the large glass-and-steel building in downtown Gotham.

But on closer look, it became clear that something was amiss on the third floor of the Gotham Diamond Exchange. On a hot night like this, why was there frost covering the windows? And why on the inside?

"Mind if I help myself?" The gravelly monotone voice broke the silence.

The question was directed at a group of security guards, each completely encased in massive chunks of ice. Mr. Freeze stomped through the room, past huge icicles that almost reached from ceiling to floor. He poured a tray of uncut diamonds into his leather satchel.

"Didn't think so," he said.

He approached a large vault door and nodded solemnly. "The choice cuts must be in the icebox."

Freeze raised his arm and gave the sealed

Batman catches an arsonist in the act.

A spectacular tackle!

"I'm Firefly. [...] Fire and fly."

Firefly blasts a Batarang out of the sky.

An awesome chase around skyscrapers!

With his jet pack, Batman easily dodges Firefly's blasts.

A fight to the finish on a high rooftop.

GOTHCORP EMPLOYEE OF THE MONTH

Firefly unmasked . . . and swatted like a bug.

An icy diamond heist in Gotham harbor.

The police think the trail's gone cold, but Batman uses infrared to track the crook.

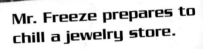

Mr. Freeze prepares to chill a jewelry store.

"Victor Fries? I thought you were dead!"

Mr. Freeze gets the drop on Batman — and turns him into a Popsicle!

An incredible escape, sliding on an ice ramp.

The odds are more even now that Batman's got his arctic Batsuit.

Which will triumph, fire or ice?

door an icy blast. With one tap of his sonic ice pick, the frozen metal shattered.

He entered the vault and marveled at the many shelves of dazzling diamonds, scooping them by the handful. "Lovely little glaciers," he murmured.

Mr. Freeze zipped up his bag and walked out of the vault — right into a flying, two-footed kick that knocked him to the ground. He pushed himself back to his feet and turned to face the dark, shadowy figure.

"Batman," said Mr. Freeze. "I thought you would never arrive."

Batman flicked open several Batarangs. "Sorry to keep you in suspense," he said as he threw them all.

Mr. Freeze reacted fast and each Batarang clanked heavily to the ground, covered in ice. "I have been looking forward to our reunion," said Freeze.

"Reunion?" Batman had no time to question him further. He dove to avoid the icy blasts that surged toward him. Snow and ice began to pile up around the room. He flipped over an ice hill to dodge another blast.

"Exercise will keep you warm only for so long," intoned Mr. Freeze. He adjusted a dial on his suit. His left palm began a wide dispersal of frozen gas and ice. With his right hand, he resumed blasts at Batman.

"Slowing, aren't we?" asked Mr. Freeze. "That would be the hypothermia setting in."

Batman stumbled away from another blast as the room continued to fill with ice and frost.

"We both recognize the symptoms," said Mr. Freeze. "Reaction time slows. Reflexes grow sluggish." The blasts kept coming. Batman shivered involuntarily. They were getting closer. "Next come the hallucinations, lack of consciousness, and finally, the *Big Chill*, old friend."

Batman launched himself at Freeze, who responded with a double blast of ice.

He jumped onto a frozen table and hurled a Batarang at a huge icicle overhead, sending the ice crashing down onto Mr. Freeze. Immediately, Batman was on him. He had Freeze's wrists in a tight grip, forcing them up so the arctic blasts shot harmlessly into the air.

Batman's gloved hands began to ice over, but they held firm. "You keep talking as if we've met," said Batman. "Mister . . . ."

He leaned in very close, finally getting a good look through the hazy mist inside

Mr. Freeze's icy helmet. Batman pulled back in shocked recognition.

"Victor Fries!?" he said in almost a whisper. "But you're — "

That moment of surprise was all Freeze needed. He slapped both hands down on Batman's shoulders and sent ice pouring over Batman's body.

"If I'm no longer living, Batman," said Freeze, "*you* are the one who iced me." Within moments, Batman was encased in ice from the neck down.

"Allow me to return the favor," intoned Freeze.

His dead-sounding laugh was enough to send an extra chill down Batman's already frozen back.

18

Batman's head lolled to one side. He whipped it upright, fighting unconsciousness. The cold was intense.

"I was just Victor Fries, common bank robber, back then," said Mr. Freeze. "But I'd hit the big-time. Diamonds. The biggest score of my *former* life."

Batman remembered the car chase that had ended so disastrously last winter. His mind numbly drifted back to that day.

He could see it so clearly: Fries's van was right ahead of him. It ran a red light and then had to turn fast to avoid hitting cars in the intersection. The van flipped and plowed through the plate-glass window of a nearby building: Cryonic Options, Inc.

Batman had seen Fries scrambling out of his seat, bag of diamonds still clutched in his hand. He'd followed him into the dark building.

Fries had fled deeper then, smashing his way into the cryobank room. Batman could still see those rows of individual cryopods, lined up like futuristic, snow-white coffins. It was a strange sight. Tubes ran from each pod, and small hazy windows showed whether the pods were empty or occupied.

"No way I'm letting some Bat-creep throw me in the cooler," yelled Fries. He pounded on a control panel, flipping switches and pressing buttons.

"Wait!" shouted Batman.

Hoses from giant tanks full of liquid nitrogen and liquid Freon whirred to life. A huge robotic arm slid across the room on a track. The arm inserted itself into a pod, then retracted and moved on to the next.

Automated hoses began filling the pods with high-pressure gas, forming ice crystals on the pod windows. Fries grabbed a hose and ripped it free, aiming the freezing gas at Batman. Electricity sizzled in the air from live wires.

Batman swept his cape around him and rolled back into the shadows. Fries stared desperately around him, pointing the hose in all directions. Sparks flew from the torn wires.

With a soft thump, Batman dropped

down behind Fries and yanked the hose out of his hands. Fries fell backwards. The robotic arm swept past, accidentally snagging the sack of diamonds.

"My diamonds!" Fries leaped onto the robotic arm, swinging out into the room.

Batman tried to pull him back but could not. "Fries, NO!"

Victor Fries sneered at Batman as he crawled along the moving arm and began to untangle his diamonds from the very end. A pod hatch opened. The arm inserted itself into the pod, along with Fries!

The arm retracted, leaving Fries stuck inside.

The hatch sealed shut on the live wires of the torn hose. Batman could see them sizzling and sparking inside the pod. He jumped onto the hatch, trying to pry it open, but was flung backward by electric shock.

He saw Fries pounding from the inside. The other hose filled the pod with frozen gas that mingled with crackling electricity.

"The icy hand of fate," intoned Mr. Freeze, "led me to that cryonics lab and inflicted the electroshock in the same instant the blood froze in my veins."

Batman snapped back out of his memories. He was still in the Gotham Diamond Exchange, encased in ice from the neck down. He struggled to stay focused.

"Was I still among the living?" asked Mr. Freeze. "My body had mutated. Neither living nor dead, I was a walking cryogenic miracle."

Gritting his teeth, Batman concentrated on Freeze's words, the only thing keeping him from drifting off into dreams.

"It didn't take much for me to motivate an 'expert in the field' to produce a suit to contain my frosty disposition," chuckled Mr. Freeze. "Until I choose to disperse it."

The quiet that settled after Freeze's sentence seemed deadly. Batman was so cold. His eyelids were so heavy.

"Thank you for creating me, Batman," said Mr. Freeze, pulling out his sonic ice pick. "Now, good-bye."

19

The door banged open. Yin and Bennett burst into the room, weapons aimed.

"Police!" shouted Yin. "Freeze!"

A faint smile played on Mr. Freeze's lips. "As you wish," he said and blasted streams of ice at the two detectives. They leaped aside.

Mr. Freeze could hear the many police sirens gathering outside. He glanced at his nearly frozen foe. "Another time, then, Batman," he said with a shrug. "Unless, of course, you simply catch your death of cold."

He quickly iced the wall behind him and shattered it with his ice pick. A gaping hole now opened out to the Gotham night. With his massive sack of diamonds in hand, Mr. Freeze jumped through. He slid down to the sidewalk on a curving ramp of ice.

Yin and Bennett rushed over and peered through the shattered wall.

"He's gone," said Bennett.

Yin turned. "But he left us a present," she said.

Trapped from the neck down in his prison of ice, Batman watched the detectives inch closer. Detective Bennett grabbed his walkie-talkie. "Bennett here: Need paramedics — *fast*."

"While we're waiting, let's take a peek," said Yin, gesturing at Batman's cowl.

"Can't say I'm not curious," replied Bennett. "Though somehow it doesn't seem right."

Yin rolled her eyes.

"Hey," Bennett said defensively. "Bats got into this pickle because he was trying to stop Freeze."

"Missing the point, Bennett. I'm sure Batman means well, I really am," said Yin. "But he's still a vigilante."

Batman listened, shivering but grimly silent. Yin turned toward him.

"And according to the law, Batman," she said as she reached toward his cowl, "that makes you a criminal, just like the rest."

"Whoa, hold up a sec, Yin," said Bennett. He pointed at an orange glow inside the ice. "What's that?"

The glow began to get brighter. Ice began to melt away from it, revealing a burning Bat-flare clutched in one of Batman's hands. Cracks began to spread across the rest of the ice-block containing Batman.

"No!" shouted Yin.

Batman fell backwards out of the ice and away from Yin's outstretched hand. He shot his Bat-grapnel and swung weakly around the detectives and through the hole in the wall. Activating his Bat-wave Transmitter with the last of his strength, he tumbled down the ice ramp painfully, spilling out into the open cockpit of the Batmobile.

Yin and Bennett stared through the hole in the building as the Batmobile roared away.

20

The Batmobile screeched to a halt safely inside the Batcave. Alfred was already waiting with a silver tray of beverages in his hand.

The hatch opened.

"Something cold to drink, sir?" asked Alfred. He stopped, aghast, when he saw the state that Bruce was in. Bruce's skin was bluish, his teeth were chattering, and he could barely hold his head up. Alfred tossed the tray aside and ran to the Batmobile.

Fifteen minutes later, he had Bruce swaddled in blankets in front of a roaring fireplace. He pulled the thermometer out of Bruce's mouth and checked it.

"One hundred four point eight," he said. "It's official, Master Bruce. You are running a fever."

Bruce was still shivering but also sweating and practically delirious. "F-Freeze," he stammered.

Alfred poured him a cup of hot tea. "This

Earl Grey will warm you."

A bead of cold sweat ran down Bruce's forehead. "N-no," he said, shivering. "*Freeze.* It's my fault he's wh-what he is."

"Master Bruce?" Alfred was concerned.

"Yin was right," said Bruce. "I'm not helping the l-law . . . I'm just breaking it." His whole body seemed to sink in defeat.

"Master Bruce, you really must get some rest."

"You were r-right, Alfred. Maybe it *is* time for Batman to take a vacation. A p-permanent one." He shuddered from the chill inside his bones.

Meanwhile, only fifteen blocks away, an alarm blared on a sun baked Gotham street. A door shattered into frozen shards and Mr. Freeze calmly walked out with more diamonds.

"Baby, it's cold outside," said Mr. Freeze, blasting snow into the air above him so it gently fell on his path as he strolled.

A police car pulled up alongside him and an officer jumped out.

"You there," shouted the young officer. "Freeze! Right where you are! I said, freeze!"

Within the Freon mist of his icy helmet, Mr. Freeze smiled.

21

Bruce huddled under the blankets, muttering to himself deliriously. His fever was still running high and he was drifting in and out of reality.

"I'm a criminal," he mumbled, "like the rest. . . . I should give it up. . . ." He pulled the blankets tighter around his shivering body.

Alfred watched him from the shadows. He couldn't take it anymore.

"Sir," he said sternly, crossing the room. "I would be more than delighted to encourage you to hang up the cape and cowl out of concern for your general health and welfare."

Alfred paused and shook his head sadly. "However," he continued, "I know you. You would only hold it against me once your fever broke and you came to your senses."

He could see that Bruce hadn't heard a word he'd said. Bruce's glazed eyes were fixed on a portrait hanging on the wall across from him. A portrait of his parents.

Bruce moaned. He was hallucinating. He was lost in an icy cavern deep under the ground. He felt small, like a child. In his dream, he wiped his cheeks clean of tears. He was lost and looking for someone, someone important.

Two large figures emerged on either side of him, taking his hands in theirs. He felt so much better, comforted by their presence. They helped him move forward through the icy cavern. Bruce looked up gratefully from his mother to his father. They smiled down at him.

Bruce suddenly realized that the cavern was actually a dark alley and he began to feel nervous. He pulled at his parents' hands, trying to hurry them along. Someone stepped out at the other end of the alley, blocking their only exit.

"Not again!" Bruce heard himself shouting in his child voice. "I won't let this happen again!"

He stared at the stranger who stepped into the light. This time, it was not the desperate face of a random mugger, the man who killed his parents in an act of thoughtless violence. This time, in the place of the real killer was Mr. Freeze.

Snow and ice swirled around him. He saw the portrait of his parents become covered over in ice and then shatter into a million shards.

He scared awake with a gasp.

Bruce looked around the room and realized he had been dreaming. He was alone and the television was on.

" . . . Mr. Freeze's crime spree continues," the glossy TV news reporter was saying. "He was last seen entering Gotham Municipal Park, but the police who followed in pursuit have yet to emerge."

Bruce wiped his forehead and pushed his blankets to the side. He turned off the television and the room darkened noticeably. A few embers glowed in the fireplace. The sky through the window was a dusky gray.

"Alfred?" Bruce called.

He sat up, swinging his legs off the couch. He stretched his arms into the air. "Alfred?"

A wall panel slid silently to the side and Alfred entered from one of the many secret Batcave passages. "Ahh, regained some of our fire, have we?" said Alfred.

Bruce stood up. He was still a little weak

but his fever had broken, and he was filled with a renewed sense of determination. "Batman is needed," he said simply.

"I figured as much," responded Alfred. "That's why I've taken the liberty of weatherproofing your suit."

Bruce stepped into the passageway with Alfred and rode down on the specialized elevator platform in silence. He murmured in appreciation as he gazed upon the modified Batsuit: extra-rugged, thermo-insulated, and white as snow.

"It's mostly technology that you've been working on," said Alfred, embarrassed. "I just had a few ideas on putting it all together."

"Thank you." Bruce smiled. "I like it. Let it snow."

"Just don't forget your cough syrup," added Alfred.

22

"We're gonna need arctic survival gear if we want to get any closer to that dome," said Detective Bennett.

The police cars had made it as far into Gotham Municipal Park as they could. The detectives were crouching against a massive snowbank to avoid the biting winds. Ice and snow swirled around a gleaming white ice dome in the center of the park, where temperatures had dropped deep below zero.

Almost soundlessly, a dark shape was suddenly speeding toward them. Yin stood up and nudged Bennett. The Batmobile!

In a blur of motion, the sleek black vehicle sped past them, climbing the snow and ice effortlessly. It disappeared into the swirling snowstorm surrounding the massive dome.

Batman quickly performed a scan of the dome and swerved his vehicle. He accelerated into a section of the dome where the ice was thinnest, smashing open an entrance for himself.

He pulled to a halt. Opening the cockpit hatch, the warm air inside turned to steam and instantly froze and fell in ice fragments back onto the seat of the Batmobile. The interior of the dome was deadeningly cold.

Batman patted his new suit appreciatively and hopped out. As he inhaled, his face mask warmed the air to a temperature his lungs could handle. His tough new boots gripped the icy surfaces. He trudged toward the middle of the dome, where he hoped to find Freeze.

His hopes were fulfilled.

Mr. Freeze sat in an oasis of cold and calm. He sprawled on an ornate throne of ice, bags of diamonds strewn all around him. He tossed several large diamonds from hand to hand.

"I see you bundled up," he intoned, watching Batman's approach. "Good. This was all too easy, the diamonds, the police — challenges for an ordinary criminal."

He tossed the diamonds to the side of his ice throne and stood up. "It's clear now that I am destined for more than this." Mr. Freeze walked down to face Batman. "After all, you've made me more than human."

"Sorry, Vic," said Batman, looking up into the ghostly haze of his helmet. "But I'm done taking credit for your handiwork. We both know you put *yourself* on ice. I'm here to bring on the thaw."

"Go on, then," mocked Freeze. "Bring it!"

Batman clicked open two Batarangs, avoiding an ice blast. He threw the Batarangs and Mr. Freeze immediately covered them in ice. They dropped to the ground at Freeze's feet. *BOOM!* The Batarangs exploded, knocking Freeze backward.

Batman scrambled up and hid behind an icy stalactite. He threw several more exploding Batarangs in long arcs so Mr. Freeze wouldn't know where they were coming from. His white suit blended in with the ice and snow, camouflaging him perfectly.

"Slick as ice, Batman," said Mr. Freeze.

His own dark suit stood out like a sore thumb against the white backdrop. He knocked down the Batarangs and covered them so deep in ice that their explosions barely shook the surface.

Now Freeze raised his arms ominously. "What you failed to realize is that I won't need to *see* you when you're buried."

Snow surged out of Mr. Freeze's palms, filling the air and piling up toward the roof. Within moments, Freeze was standing in a valley, with large hills of snow on either side of him growing at an alarming rate.

23

Batman needed to act fast. He fired his Bat-grapnel and swung across the dome, distracting Mr. Freeze from filling the dome with snow. Instead, Freeze shot off ice blasts at Batman as he soared overhead.

One huge blast headed right at him. Batman jumped onto the blast as it hit the wall, creating a newly frozen ice ramp that led right back to Mr. Freeze. Batman clicked a button on his Utility Belt and compact skis telescoped out of the bottom of his boots. He swooshed down the ramp toward Mr. Freeze, gaining speed as he slid.

Freeze threw a wall of ice up to block Batman, but exploding Batarangs took care of it and Batman burst through. Mr. Freeze held his ground.

"Your time is past, Batman," he said. "I'm king of the mountain, the new emperor of Gotham." He blasted snow and ice at Batman. "So get used to the weather."

Batman used his thick cape to repel the blow. "No, Freeze," he replied. "Gotham is *not* up for grabs."

In one smooth maneuver, Batman dropped his cape and pulled a flamethrower from his side, meeting Freeze's icy blast with a fiery one of his own.

The two elements collided explosively. Fire and ice pushed against each other, evenly matched at first. But then Mr. Freeze leaned in, concentrating, and his snowy blast began to drive the flame back toward Batman.

"Law of Thermodynamics," said Mr. Freeze. "Cold always triumphs over heat."

"It's more complicated than that," replied Batman, pressing some buttons on his Bat-wave Transmitter as his flamethrower began to sputter out.

The Batmobile roared to life and burst out of a snowbank nearby. It zoomed up an icy hill and flew toward them. Landing between the two adversaries, it began to skid on the ice, spinning around until it came to a stop against the far wall, facing away from Mr. Freeze.

Mr. Freeze spread his arms, smug with the apparent miss. He gave a small, monotone chuckle. "Two words, Batman: *snow tires*."

Batman grinned. He clicked another button on his transmitter and the Batmobile revved its engine, huge blue flames blasting Mr. Freeze from the rear of the vehicle.

Freeze was knocked across the dome, crashing into a pillar that supported the whole structure. With a brutal crack, chunks of the roof began to crumble in huge, dangerous slabs of ice. Mr. Freeze fell hard to the ground, out cold.

Batman waited for the roof to stabilize. He stood over Freeze for a moment, looking into the villain's cold, blank face, and then he hopped into the Batmobile.

Already, a helicopter was approaching one of the gaping holes in the icy dome. Outside, the swirling ice storm had ended. Yin and Bennett clung to a rope ladder that lowered toward Freeze's unconscious body.

Batman fired up the Batmobile and plowed through the opening he'd made earlier.

Detective Bennett stared at the scene. "Bats may be a criminal," he said. "But he's *my* kind of criminal."

24

The Batmobile slid to a halt on a glowing blue platform in the bowels of the Batcave.

Alfred was ready for him. When the hatch hissed open, he held up his silver tray. This time, a teapot steamed beside a small wrapped oval.

"Hot tea and a lozenge, sir?" he asked.

Bruce pulled off his weatherproof cowl and mask. He considered for a second. "Cold drink on a warm beach?" he replied.

Alfred smiled. "Certainly, sir. I'll just — "

The Bat-wave alarm echoed through the cave. Both men glanced up toward the Bat-console they knew was blinking.

"Another time, then," said Alfred. They walked together to a floor panel that began to rise, taking them up to the console.

Something new had disturbed the Gotham night.

Not for long.